spiderseed

David Hartley

First edition, 2016

ISBN 978-1-5262-0109-6

PRINTED IN THE UNITED KINGDOM

Published by Sleepy House Press
248 Upper Chorlton Road,
Manchester, M16 0BJ

sleepyhousepress.com

Sleepy House Press is a not-for-profit writing community, online journal, feedback workshop and (now) print publishers based in Manchester.

This collection is dedicated to Nici West, Dan Carpenter, Joe Daly and Fat Roland of Bad Language in Manchester.

Their peerless dedication to championing and showcasing new writing is second to none and it has been an honour and a privilege to speak my words on their stages over the past five years.

Thanks Bad Language for giving me the platform, the encouragement, and the audiences. You guys are the most precious of peoples.

Contents

Trails 09

Pickaxe 13

The Librarian 15

Tower Defence 23

From the Deepest Depth 25

Trade 31

St. Joseph's 33

Unicorn Logistics 37

Fly 39

Most Haunted 45

Pulse.. 47

Smiling Fish.. 53

Spiderseed.. 57

Scientists 61

Age Concern... 63

Caught.. 71

Trust the Tiles.. 73

The Cleaner.. 77

Twitchy Leg 81

Explanations 83

Acknowledgments 87

Trails

The slugs made an outline of a body with their trails.
I mopped it up and put down pellets. What if the neighbours saw?

The next day, the pellets dodged, the outline was back. And around the perimeter of the patio, a cordon of dew-drenched web. The scene glistened in the dawn light. I felt sick. I snapped the webs, scrubbed away the body and covered the slabs in salt.

As the afternoon waned I perched in the window and looked out. I watched ants clear away the salt grains while snails settled in to mark evidence. Ladybirds clustered where the blood had splattered and butterflies fluttered at dust to find fingerprints. The cordon reappeared, thicker this time, and I spotted a triumphant beetle hoist an errant hair then stash it in his thorax before scuttling away.

Wasps set up a nest on the shed wall and patrolled. Passing bees rubbernecked and were buzzed off; no news for the hive, not yet.

As night finally fell, out came the slugs. Eight fat smears of viscera; they pulsed from every crack and hole and mulched together into one squelching mass. The blob retraced the drawing: the back first, then the head with the snout of the mouth, then the chest and the four legs and the final curve of the tail. The ladybirds fluttered by the neck and slowly pooled out. The wasps landed and closed their wings, the snails stayed in their shells. I watched the slugs bleed back into the shadows and stared, and stared, and stared at the scene until it became too dark to see.

As I turned from the window I saw the jitter of a spider shoot from darkness to darkness across the floor. A moth settled on the lamp and dimmed the room.

Somewhere by the bed, a hornet buzzed. I felt hollow. I felt weak.

I knelt down, put my hands on my head, closed my eyes and waited.

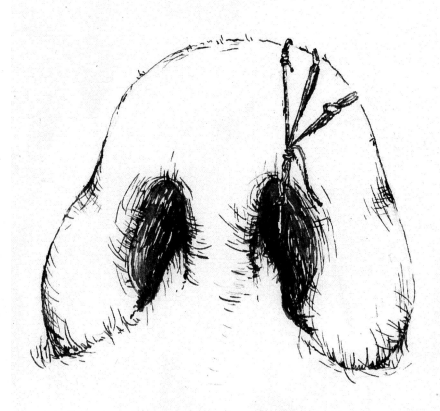

Pickaxe

I pause for breath outside my own nostril. Last night I dreamt you died and the dream clings to my brain like a limpet; my wet cheeks, the embarrassment of grief. I can't concentrate, I need it gone.

So I heave the pickaxe onto my shoulder and ready the rope. I'm heading in.

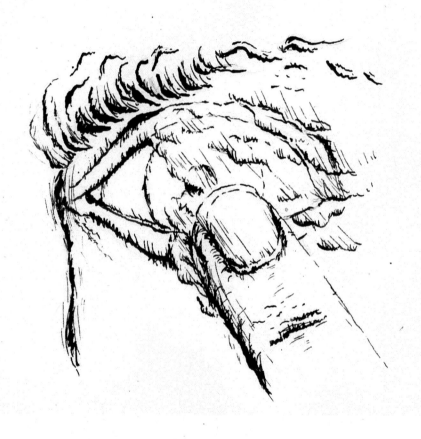

The Librarian

It takes him days to arrange the books into their positions.
The timelines and date-stamps have to be precisely aligned
and the editions properly stacked and balanced. The
pages must be pinned open along a delicate sequence of
primes and all the science fiction must be locked away in
the lead-lined vault. He turns the statues to face the track-
lines of their relevant histories and covers their eyes with
wax. He adjusts the blinds until the light-level is just right;
this is best when a gibbous moon is slightly risen and the
sun is just about to disappear. Too much dust interferes
with the transit so the place must be spotlessly clean, but
this is the simplest chore because he never allows too
much dust. And finally, he must be mindful of himself
as the helmsman: so, for the final hour, while he awaits
the lunar-rise and the solar-fall, he mediates among the

children's books. When all is correct, when every element is just right, his library becomes a time machine.

The doors crash open as the aNoNs let themselves in. The librarian does not allow his muscles to tense up. It will be better this time. It will come to an end. For their final journey the location is his choice. He opens his eyes, adjusts the *Gruffalo* display and walks calmly to the Reading Room. He emerges on the balcony and watches them for a while, their faces plasticked into permanent Guy Fawkes grins. They scour the console, try to discover their destination. The librarian descends via French History and pulls out the tome he needs.

'What you got for us, Banks?' barks aNoN58446 as the librarian steps into the hall. The others lurk behind him, smirks cocked and a dullness behind lenses that flicker through the constant web.

Without a word he crosses to the opposite alcove

and pulls out the costume basket. He flips it open and they dive in. While they dress up he sets the Napoleon biography in place and pins open pages 154-155. The console locks on and he adjusts the dials to read the correct passage. The execution of the Duc D'Engien.

'What is it?' hisses aNoN90797. 'Firing squad?' The voice is strained through the transfixed lips.

'You'll see,' says the librarian.

They have dredged themselves from the murkiest heap of the darknet, where the goaders and cowards hide, where dignity and empathy lie ripped and tortured. Somehow they found him and his library and now they own him, and his library. Unlimited use, unlimited access or they'll flick their crooked fingers and tear the house down. He agreed, of course. How could he resist those smiles? But the control is his, the knowledge is his and the past is strictly Read Only, no changes.

So this is where they have their fun. They use his library to travel back and watch famous executions. Just for kicks. They've seen Joan burn, Anne lose her head and Saddam hang. And worse. They can only pick what the books describe but there's plenty to keep them entertained. Each of the six picked a death — each more horrible than the last — and the Librarian played along, practiced his deviant grin in the mirror. They took him for a convert. Today, he's the seventh to choose.

The console bleeps its readiness and aNoN66997 squeals and claps. The librarian flicks the switch. The library is silent but they are on their way.

He turns to face them. The dragoon coats and helmets look ridiculous but he no longer cares.

'The year is 1804,' he says. 'The place is Chateau de Vincennes. A duke by the name of Louis Antoine has been dragged from his home by dragoons, tried on trumped-up charges of treason, and is about to be executed by firing squad in the moat of the castle.'

aNoN90797 punches the air and cheers. They high-five and hug. The librarian feels hollow.

'The duke is almost certainly innocent.' More celebration. 'His death will send shockwaves around Europe. It is the moment, they say, when Napoleon went from being a valiant emperor to despotic tyrant. It is the beginning of his end.'

'Who's Napoleon?' rasps aNoN90797.

The books flutter as the library lands. The librarian pushes the grin to his face and raises his hand to indicate the door. His other hand grips the edge of the console like he's holding on for dear life.

The aNoNs bound out. He follows them with weakening knees to the door and watches as they bound over a twilight field to the castle beyond. They don't look back so he abolishes the grin, shuts the door and runs back to the console. He flings out the biography and slots his journal in place. He gets a fix on his scrawled predictions and fine-tunes the dials. His hands run cold, his lips twitch, but his focus is sharp. The books flutter again and, after an achingly long pause, the console bleeps. He hits the switch and tears away from 19th century France, back to his own time.

The library settles as it lands. If it is angry at him it doesn't say so. The books close like eyes drooping to sleep. He looks at the door. Would the world be much changed? He wonders, not for the first time, about the laws of time travel. He wonders if he should write them, or if he already has somehow.

He shuts the console down and locks it away. He takes the Napoleon biography, finds a quiet corner, and reads.

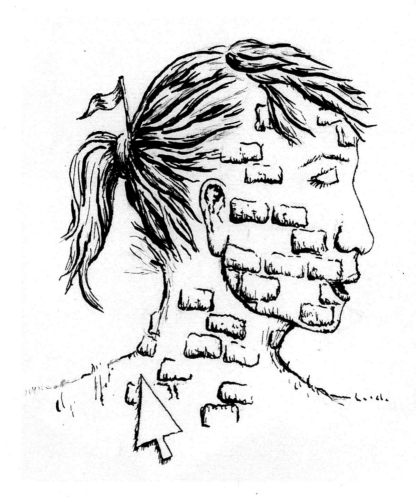

Tower Defence

She left half way through her move, half way through the game, with her block half way out of the tower.

The militia are stationed in the holes. No-one allowed in or out.

The commander guards her block. It is his alone. Precarious and precious. He perches on the end and watches the stars and the clouds. He has a fiancé at home, faithful and lonely, but proud.

She plays Farmville now, but not with me.

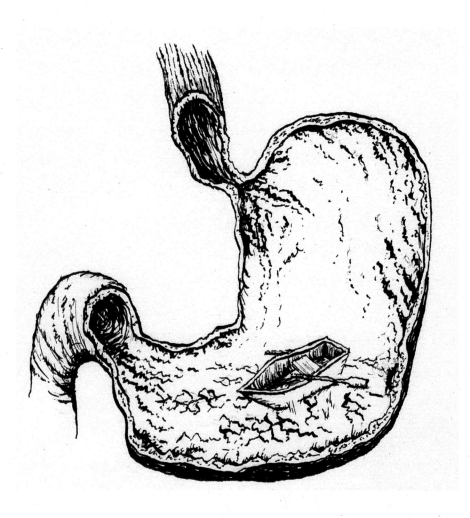

From the Deepest Depth

The man smelled of squid guts and dead salt. There were white flecks in his beard and his fingernails were crinkled like fragments of shell. His eyes would not meet mine. They darted around in their sockets, minnows in rock pools.

'Thanks for seeing me,' he said. He held out the vial. 'This is it.'

Thick, clouded glass stopped with a cork. Liquid inside which looked dark, but it could have been the tint of the glass, hard to tell. There was a space on the table for acquisitions and I had my gloves on ready, but he kept a tight hold.

'Thanks for bringing it in. Take your time.'

'Don't want nothin' for it.' Spit foamed at the corner of his lips. 'Nothin.'

'A donation?'

He nodded.

'Very generous.'

That seemed to soothe him. He wiped his mouth, scratched his chin, readied himself.

'It's water,' he said, 'From the deepest depth.'

'From where?'

'The deepest depth. The deepest point of the deepest place. From the bottom of the Mariana Trench.'

I frowned. His breaths thickened, his grip on the vial tightened.

'Please,' I said, indicating the table.

'You be careful?' Dart, dart, dart went the eyes.

'Of course.'

'Don't open it. Promise me.'

'I promise.'

He set it down like he was placing a landmine. I took

it into my hands with just as much care. It was nothing. Just a small vial containing a small amount of liquid which could have just as easily come from the tap in the men's toilets in the foyer. No marks on the glass, nothing on the cork, no labels or stamps.

'Deepest depth,' he muttered. His eyes were fixed now, right on mine, circles in circles in circles. I was, for that moment, held and then, a moment later, swept in.

'I'm sure we can find a place,' I said.

He nodded. A small smile, to himself. Another nod and then: 'Thanks.'

He turned on his heel and marched away. As he wrestled with the door to get out of Collections, his coat knocked against the wall. Tinkle, tinkle, clink, clink; he swore, put a hand against the bulging pocket to stop the sound, then barged his way to freedom. The door clicked shut. The smell stayed.

I ran my finger around the edge of the cork, round and round and round. I didn't want to look at the vial again. I would find a place for it.

I didn't move for a while. It was raining outside, I was quite sure, a heavy downpour. And the pipes of the museum were flush and full, like blood vessels of some giant body forever thirsty. And in my own body; my mouth an arid desert, my stomach a dried-up lake. A bead of sweat burst from my forehead, streaked down my cheek to feed my lips then seeped its way to my tongue. It was salty, it was precious and it was gone too soon.

Trade

I swear the merchant laughed as I handed him my tibia.

He chucked the whole bone through his Grender. The

machine clanged as it charged, sputtered through a scan

and then spat out a green flag. Genuine human, approved

for sale. Only then did he glance at my stump, another

chuckle playing across his face.

He took his time finding Sasha. I'd hoped she would

be thrashing at the bars to get out but she just sat there,

sad eyes, obvious ribs. I glared at the merchant but said

nothing.

It didn't matter really. I'd saved her some meat.

St Joseph's

He set himself to burying every part of St. Joseph's
beneath its floor within the caverns of the catacombs. He
removed the decor first, the candelabra, the carpets, the
statuettes of the saints, and gave them simple wooden
headstones carved from benches.

He followed this with the seating and the vestments
and the objects of mass, along with his own sceptre and
mitre and all the Bibles. With the room clear he took
down the windows, carefully aimed stones bringing out
each stained fragment like a fall of winter petals.

An earthquake – a retaliation perhaps – brought
down much of the east wall, which he set to burying as
soon as it was safe to approach. Not long after, the beams
and struts of the ceiling failed and the elements poured in.
There was just enough room left below to fit in the roof

rubble but he set a few of the smallest chunks aside to serve as further headstones.

Finally, he dug graves for the congregation, who had slumped into their decays, awaiting the completion of his project. Flakes of flesh fell from bones as he carried each body to its designated place. The name of each parishioner slipped out of his lips to be swallowed into the howl of the wind. He whispered each into their rest, invented new prayers, folded them into brief and painless eulogies. He left the graves unmarked.

Only the bell tower remained so he shut himself in and watched the sky. And, with silence and grace, with patience and defiance, with crumbled hands and a quivering neck, he awaited a response.

It came soon after.

Unicorn Logistics

A great gust of jungle air sweeps through the cargo bay as there; the doors open, but my blood does not get warmer because then, at that very moment, I first properly hear the clippety-clop of angry hooves on concrete and soon, within mere moments, I will encounter the split second of my duty and now, in my hands, the giant cork feels very, very heavy.

Fly

When Fly died they cut through the walls and pulled me back to Admin. She was crouched in the corner behind pencils pilfered from desks, neatly lined up in a size-order curve.

She calmed down when she realised it was me. She gathered the pencils and stuffed them into her pockets. I didn't dare argue and shot a look to the Staff to say they shouldn't either. They sliced us back to the Wilson house, eyes averted, faces blank.

'Good to see you, Fly,' I said, with all the right tones.

'Buzz buzz,' she said, soothed.

*

'Don't know what to do.'

I let her zigzag the room in the lazy circles that earned her the nickname. Her statement was not directed at me.

It was part of the process, part of the figuring out.

I let myself wonder how she died. Painful or quick? Her own fault or no-one's? I thought about Mum and Dad, arranging another funeral. Then I shut it all out of my mind. A distant world, another life. Irrelevant. Fly stopped buzzing and turned away. Now the question was asked, not with words but with her stance.

'I'll show you what to do,' I said.

*

Night fell and the Wilson family buried into their beds. Worried Staff sliced peepholes from Admin, which didn't help with my own nerves.

'Let's do some colouring-in.'

She froze, her eyes diagonal-right as she processed my statement.

'Hard or easy?'

'Easy,' I said, the only possible response.

We started with Jim, the father. I dropped the sheen over his left eyelid and showed Fly how to do the same to his right. She was very gentle.

'We're going to draw his dreams,' I said. A flutter of panic. I called up the stylus before she could react and the sight of the instrument stilled her. I let her take it and called up another for myself.

'It's very easy. Put the pencil into his ear and I'll tell you what to draw. Watch me.'

I slipped my stylus into Jim's left ear and the nib appeared behind the sheen. Today Jim's boss had told him all about his skiing trip and it had made Jim jealous. I drew a sandcastle, a deck chair, a holiday brochure.

'Please draw a boat, Fly.' Jim loves fishing.

She shoved her stylus in and giggled while she sketched out triangle sails, a rectangle deck and big, smiling, circle sun.

*

The next morning the Wilsons woke to a Saturday and gathered for breakfast, eager to grasp the colours of their dreams. They talked about plans for the summer.

Fly was crouched in the corner, no pencils. She buzzed out a story to her fingers, told them their dreams perhaps. She'd been in a happy mood last night. It wasn't going to always be that easy, but it was a damn good start.

'Good to see you, Fly,' I said.

'Buzz buzz.'

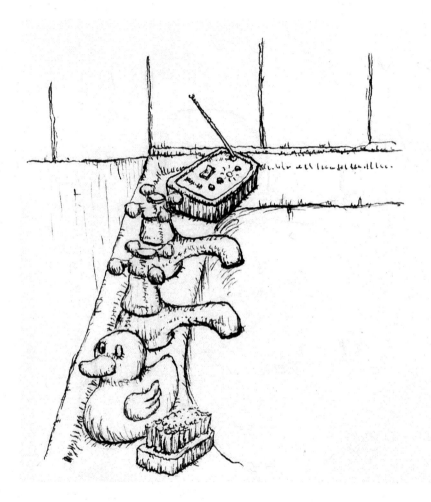

Most Haunted

Every night,

at 2:30am,

Derek Acorah

climbs into your bath,

and masturbates.

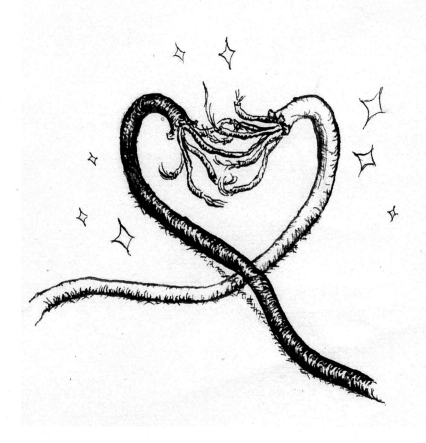

Pulse

My head is a blow-dryer, my voice is hot air. Setting one for yes, setting two for no.

'Can I ask you something?' says John through his mobile-phone hand.

Setting one. A gentle blast from my snout becomes steam, curls up into the grey sky and fades off. John hesitates. I unravel a wire and flap it across the ground to him. He lets one of his come loose and we entwine.

'Be honest,' he says.

Honesty, I want to say. How can we be anything but honest now? Souls reduced to electrons, minds that crackle like static, blackouts whenever the sun flares. My left arm is an alarm clock, my right arm a lamp, my torso a small TV, and I stutter around on a pair of straighteners. If there are any liars left in the world I'll burn them to death with these legs.

I click again. *Yesssss* hums my soft breath.

'Do you want this? I mean *really* want it?'

I look at him with my light bulb. His body is his beloved PlayStation, his head our widescreen TV. The image is stuck on what it showed when the Pulse struck: a cockpit of some fighter spaceship about to destroy an enemy. He can't change it no matter how hard he tries. His emotion is permanently poised on that cartoon moment of kill or be killed.

He doesn't turn to me. His bulb watches the scene ahead. 'Flesh and blood again. Spit and bone, toenails and hair. Wrinkles and hiccups and bruises and itches.'

Frowns and smiles, winks and tears. Being able to jump, stretch, dance, sleep. A voice.

I look back. Down in the valley, at the front of the queue, emancipation is promised. Six scientists with 3D printer bodies. They feed on animal corpses and spool out new structures: skeleton to skin and every delicate intricacy in between. Holes are left in skulls for sockets, fixed into place by a person with drill-bit fingers and a car battery for a head. The first new human body is nearly ready, a male of course, but they look like they're having trouble finishing the eyes.

Snaking down the hillside, a thousand thousand bulbs throw jittery spotlights onto this lifeless Adam, expectant but wondering. Excited but worried. Smartphone voices politely litter the air, unable to use anything close to the correct tone.

John's bulb turns to me. He wants an answer. Do I want to go back? We've not had enough time to live this through yet; we've not told stories, not fought wars, not rearranged loves or faced fears. The animal corpses look freshly slaughtered. I've heard if you strip off insulation you can fuse with another, sparks and bolts, cracks and

bangs. Dangerous, perhaps, but imagine the orgasm.

My wire strokes along John's, expectant but

wondering. I turn to him and click to setting two. My no

blasts like freedom and we stutter away.

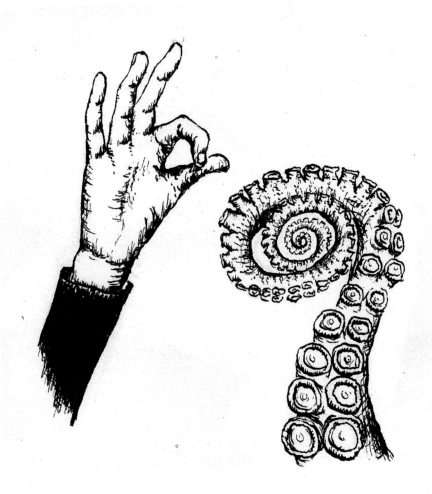

Smiling Fish

They have to look friendly, said the brief. *Happy to be touched. The sharks can look a bit menacing but not too much. We'd rather not fix anything in Photoshop.*

So they dunked him in the biggest tank, full gear. All the hand signals learnt and a team on standby in case he needed to be hoisted away from stinging tails or snapping jaws. The creatures swept out of the gloom for a quick look before jolting away. So much smaller this side of the magnified glass.

He snapped and snapped, caught a goofy manta ray, the wise grin of a bold turtle. The smiles annoyed him. He wondered what they meant. Wondered what the fish should be so damn pleased about. They didn't act relaxed, didn't act like they wanted to be touched.

So when the hammerhead snapped his tether, he

didn't panic. Instead, he stowed his camera, picked a ray and followed it.

There was an exit at the base of the tank where clown fish manned a security door. They waved him through.

Outside, a queue of shimmering shoals trailed through the coral; two orcas kept the peace. An octopus in a shipwreck ticket booth waggled its tentacles at him. The octopus wasn't smiling. He tried an 'OK' sign, then a 'thumbs up'. The octopus rolled its eyes, then camouflaged.

The ray found a quiet home for him, a niche at the base of the reef.

Spiderseed

Da was mad when I came home with Spiderseed. He
shouted I coulda got Butterfly, Hamster, somethin' nice,
but I couldna, not with six coin an' half. He's not been
down seedmarket for moons; coin don't stretch as far as
he thinks no more. But I did'n say nothin'; just watched
while he took the seed and crushed it in his salty hands.
Kept one back tho', stashed in my secret pocket, where it
stayed until he gave me my play-out again.

Spiderseed grows fast. I counted moons: three full
ones, four curves, then two more days before the first
curling leg began to reach from a knot in the branch.
I touched its tip with my finger. Da thinks I'm weird
liking bugs and insects; calls me a disappointment when
he knows I can hear. But I can't like Giraffewoods or
Hippoaks or Lemurlarch cus we can't buy 'em. I only likes

the things we can afford. Maybes that's what makes Da so mad.

I touched the tip again. It curled back then found a grip on the bark. Soon, with pulling, another leg appeared, then another, then a bit of body. I left it be; let it find its own way to its own life.

Tomorrow the tree gonna be wriggling with 'em. Then one more moon and they'll start to spin up webs. I've read it: they'll string the silk between the branches like lines in glass. They'll shatter the sky and bring down the stars, catch the moon, cocoon it.

And if Da thinks that's scrat I'll tell him; maybes they'll catch a Butterfly as well, maybes two, and then he can have all the seeds he really wants.

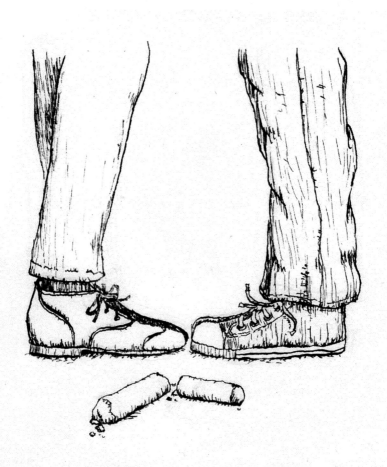

Scientists

Their first date, the cinema. A film about scientists and theories, but mostly about love and triumph. He wanted to say: the movies can never explain science. The maths, the physics; it's too complex, too involved, too beyond most people. Symbols on giant blackboards, snapped chalk, a few long nights. Then one transition from frustration to revelation and crack! the ground broken, mankind enhanced, all in the crunch of a handful of popcorn. Nothing learnt but everything felt.

This was his first date with a man. He wanted to hold a hand, if not the one beside him now then one from the near future. He let the film tell him its story. He shared the popcorn.

Age Concern

Ry left her the spot in his will. He made sure the company owned it and kept it safe, just for her. She never went back, not in reality, not to Earth-proper. But now Saskia was pregnant with her third and there was just enough time left to make one last trip. That was the place. That's where she wanted to be when Age Concern came.

She disconnected the suite as best she could and scheduled a valuation, giving the bots a few free hours of roaming in the manner that had always made her smile. Gliding figurines skimming over prime floor space, like privileged Victorians on frozen lakes. She tricked herself into pretending they would stay like that forever. Maybe they would.

The shuttle took her in-world to the London platforms, to Juliet first, which, like everywhere else, had long lost the serenity she remembered but it was a good place to stock up on chip-supplies for her suit. Then she rode the cascades, down past Jubilee, Glasto and the Net islands, refusing to disembark despite the best efforts of the hustlers at each dock. After Olympic she managed to grab a seat and didn't leave it until the spires of Plymouth were swallowed back into the clouds and the carriage clicked her onto dry land. Back in dear old England. She looked up: the St George sky stretched out above her like a forcefield.

She queued for Ry's Plymouth gravetag and phoned up Saskia so they could mutter nothings of remembrance to the Age Concern slideshow. Saskia took the opportunity to make her apologies, which were a bit bloody late now but easily waved away. They hadn't physically seen each other in ten years; the girl was nothing more than highly polished pixilation, shrunk or stretched depending on the screen of choice.

The last of her savings went on a car hire: an old 2020s Ford with five seats and manual controls, but she let the satellites do the driving. It was nice to feel the bump and swerve of wheels again. She told her suit not to regulate her for a while and let the rhythms of the journey lull her to a final sleep. She woke at the border of Scotland and watched with mild interest as St George gave way to St Andrew, neither looking particularly strong in the pink fades of the September sun.

It was full night when she reached what was left of the Cairngorms. Despite its complaints, she shut down and peeled off her suit and left it in the boot of the car. In its place she put on hiking gear. Proper togs: fleece, gloves, boots, hat. She slipped Ry's old map into its laminate pocket and tied the pocket to her belt.

Tourists grinned and nodded at her as she stalked

through outer Perth. She grumbled with Ry's curses at the bagpipe classics bleating out of the tartan shops, pinning her ears with frustrating precision. Twenty-four hour tat. They seemed to have doubled in number since she was last here.

Eventually she left them behind and reached the peak of Ben Macdhui where she paid a reduced ticket price to see the view. It held her for half an hour before she spat at it for being too cluttered. The attendant gave her an odd look which set off her hiccups and giggles. Ry was with her then, she felt, chuckling along in approval.

She took the Eastern descent where at last she was rid of other people. The road down crumbled into a footpath which snaked towards the valley and ended at the gateway to the Foxbolt Preservation. Her thumbprint opened the doors but it also sent an alert to Age Concern. She didn't have long left, but she didn't need long now.

A creaky railbus took her through the forests and then up a slow climb to the abandoned observation deck. From here it was a short walk through springy heather to the X marked on Ry's map. Not that she needed to consult it; her feet knew the way.

Here she stopped. She closed her eyes and breathed in the clean air. It made her head keel and jump but the pure taste of it was glorious. Not a synthetic note, not a hint of human. She peeked one eye and positioned herself in line with the strip of pines that funnelled down the valley. Then she opened both eyes fully and stood perfectly still.

Not a thing. Not one manmade thing. The stars above, the mountain to her right, the trees to her left, the sloping meadow below. She didn't dare to turn her head to hunt the view like Ry used to; it had been too many years since she had last stood here and she had no trust left in the rest of the world. But in this spot, standing like this, it was perfect.

And then, after only fifteen minutes, the air began to thrum so she closed her eyes. The Age Concern aero dropped in from above, projecting down its sounds to announce its presence. She let it come while keeping the image of the view fixed in her mind.

The autopilot announced her name, ID number and age and awaited her confirmation. The tone of its voice was firm but pleasant. She had nothing to fear, it seemed to say, nothing to fear at all.

Caught

Halfway through the train crash, I caught the girl's eyes. She had panicked, ripped them out and flung them through that collapsing space in the blind hope that someone, somewhere, would find them, cherish them and remember her. She was lucky that day, as was I.

I keep them in a glass cabinet in the kitchen and look at them while I do the washing up.

Trust the Tiles

They will let the Scrabble tiles decide the baby's name. Seems proper for them, seems right.

Could be anything, he says.

Trust the tiles, she says. Her eyes glow, her grin is fragile.

They lay out the board on the nursery floor and set the mobile turning. It tinkles its tune like a siren's call.

Eyes closed, she says.

How many?

Until it feels right.

He closes his eyes and reaches into the bag. The tiles feel like vertebrate, like fossils, like money. He takes them out one at a time. He stops after tile four. Did it feel right?

Ok.

They look.

DEED

She frowns. Worry cracks her. His hand is back in the

bag, his fingers clutch another bone. He brings it out

P

and lays it down. Three more. Now it feels right.

OLL

Her waters break. They call the baby Polly.

The Cleaner

Darren took her dreamcatcher and hung it upside down above his bed. He swallowed two sleeping tablets with a shot of Night Nurse, put on his *Kiss Me* blindfold and squeaked earplugs into place. He slept for nearly sixteen hours.

The next day, with Sarah's help, he returned it. Tilly hadn't slept, as instructed. Her friends had thrown an impromptu Eurovision party, all loudspeakers and sugar highs. Her skin was cataract pale, the garland of maps around her neck stained with splatters of Red Bull. Darren watched her liver spots swirl like something out of Fantasia as Sarah passed the dreamcatcher back.

'Did it work?'

Darren managed a nod.

'Hold on, I'll get your money.'

An eternity passed. Sarah squeezed his hand. The curtain twitched and two sleepy faces peered out. One face was the Croatian flag, the other Iceland.

The money came gently to his lap, almost unnoticed. Rolled up banknotes. It felt like a drug deal.

'Thank you so much,' she whispered.

He managed another nod. Sarah pressed his hand around the drip and wheeled him away. The street passed by in a blur, but he could feel its shadowed places. He let himself close his eyes; gave himself that relief, just this once, just to rest his heavy lids. Sarah didn't notice until it was too late.

He fell asleep and dreamt of nothing.

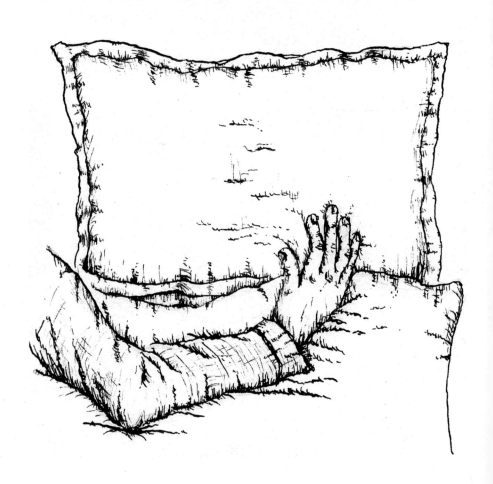

Twitchy Leg

We struggle to fall asleep together because of your Restless Legs Syndrome, or twitchy leg as we call it.

But now I can't sleep at all because I miss your Restless Legs Syndrome, or twitchy leg as we used to call it.

Explanations

Me and her and the dying dog, huddled on the deckchair,
guarding each other from the whips and bites of autumn
dropping to winter. I explain how tides work. Try to make
it a story, epic and sweeping, like some creation myth,
but the scientist inside me can't help but force my lips to
the straight and narrow. She doesn't understand, and that
hurts.

    The dog shivers, one of its last. On the wall of the
beach hut, red and yellow leaves have slipped through
cracks and found their way into the relative warmth. To
hide with us, perhaps; just as defiant, just as fragile. She's
taken one from the floor and twirls it between finger and
thumb. Fragments of its body fall with every spin, lost
against the dark sand. When she drops it, I explain climate
change. Try to make it a story, melancholic and grand, like

some symphony, but it all sounds too big and impossible, too overblown. She doesn't understand, and I suppose that's for the best.

The lantern fades and the hut goes silver. There's a super moon tonight but we won't see it. I consider explaining it: orbital fluctuations, the music of the spheres. But silence has come and we're past all that now.

I squeeze the pair of them tight against my chest and close my eyes. I can hear the ocean. The tides are coming in.

Acknowledgements

'Trails' first appeared on The MacGuffin.

'Pickaxe' first appeared in Battery Pack Volume One, packaged with issue 38 of Neon Magazine.

'The Librarian' was written in response to the E.L Burney collection of curios housed in the John Ryland's Library in Manchester. The items in the collection belonged to Isabella Banks, author of *The Manchester Man*.

'Tower Defence' was first published on The Paragraph Planet

'From the Deepest Depth' won the Live at LICA Museum of Water Flash Fiction competition and was published on Litfest.com

'Trade' was first featured as the winner of the Scrolls Flash

Fiction Challenge on the Geek Syndicate podcast.

'St. Joseph's' was first published in Scraps: The National Flash Fiction Day Anthology 2013.

'Unicorn Logistics' first appeared on thepygmygiant.com and is the oldest story in this collection.

'Fly' first appeared on the First Draft Manchester blog.

'Pulse' was shortlisted for the 'Cockpit/Blow-Dryer/ Honesty' Mash Stories competition in 2014.

'Spiderseed' was first published in the charity anthology Re:Imagined by the What I See When I Look At project. It was inspired by the picture 'Spider Branches'.

'Scientists' was first published on spelkfiction.com

'Age Concern' first appeared in the short story book which accompanies the album 'Openings' by Aka Hige.

It was published again in issue one of spontaneity.org

'The Cleaner' first appeared on The MacGuffin.

'Explanations' was first published in the Fall 2014 edition of From the Depths (Haunted Waters Press).

My thanks extend, as ever, to my long-suffering writing group Abi Hynes, Rob Cutforth, Benjamin Judge, Tom Mason, Fat Roland and Dan Carpenter for forcing me to confront the terrors inside my stories and either dig them out or make them more terrifying.

About the Author

David Hartley is a writer and performer born and raised in Preston, now based in Manchester. He writes unsettling tales about shadows, monsters and twisted futures to alarm, distract and amuse anyone who cares to read them.

His longer fiction is just as weird and has been published in various places including Structo, The Alarmist, Shooter, Foxhole and two Boo Books anthologies.

He can often be found haunting the spoken word stages of Manchester and runs his own spoken word night in Stretford called Speak Easy.

His favourite book is *Frankenstein*. His favourite animal is rabbit. His favourite colour is green. His favourite film is *Blade Runner*. His favourite reader is you.

About the Artist

Mostly Emmy does pictures for other people's words,
although sometimes she writes and performs her own.
On the internet she lives at emmyingle.weebly.com; in her
head she lives in a fairy-tale forest; in the real world she
lives in Lancaster where she is slowly stumbling her way
through university.

A word from Sleepy House Press

Hi! Sorry for planting ourselves in your new book's bum like this. We couldn't help ourselves. 'Spiderseed' is the first "real live book with pages" we've published and it's a "real live book with pages" we're immensely proud of.

When David approached us, a few months back, with idea of publishing his next collection we jumped on the idea with little to no idea of what we were doing, partly because we'd been crushing on him for ages, but mainly because we're a bunch of idiots.

Seeing 'Spiderseed' come together: David's dark, dizzying stories, Emily's pitch-perfect and (frankly) beautiful illustrations; seeing others giving a proper shit about what these artists do, running with their ideas, turning them into something lasting; it's been... well it's just been a joy.

So, firstly, we'd like to thank all our friends: Marg, Raz, Alex, Ryan, Oliver, Imo and the guys at Comma Press; we couldn't have done it without you.

And, secondly, we want to make it clear that we aren't finished. The profits from 'Spiderseed' are going straight back into our next project for local writing, and the profits from that will go into the next.

And you can help. Yes, you. We love help. So, whether you're a reader, a writer, a PR Guru, an artist or just a keen bean, we want to hear from you.

The Sleepy House is a big house and there's plenty of room.

 sleepyhousepress.com

 sleepyhousepress

 sleepyhousepress

 zzzhousepress

Further Reading

Threshold (Gumbo Press, 2013)

The first collection of haunting flash fictions by David Hartley.

Ghosts and monsters, warped realities and lost souls. Stories from the blurred edges and the dark corners.

Available on the Kindle.

Merry Gentlemen (Self published, 2014)

Fourteen twisted Christmas tales of yuletide woe.

These are the whispers in Santa's nightmares. This is *Silent Night* played backwards. The black hole of Bethlehem. Manger danger. Christmas with a capital X. Be good.

For goodness sake.

Limited copies in print. Available on the Kindle.

davidhartleywriter.com

@DHartleyWriter